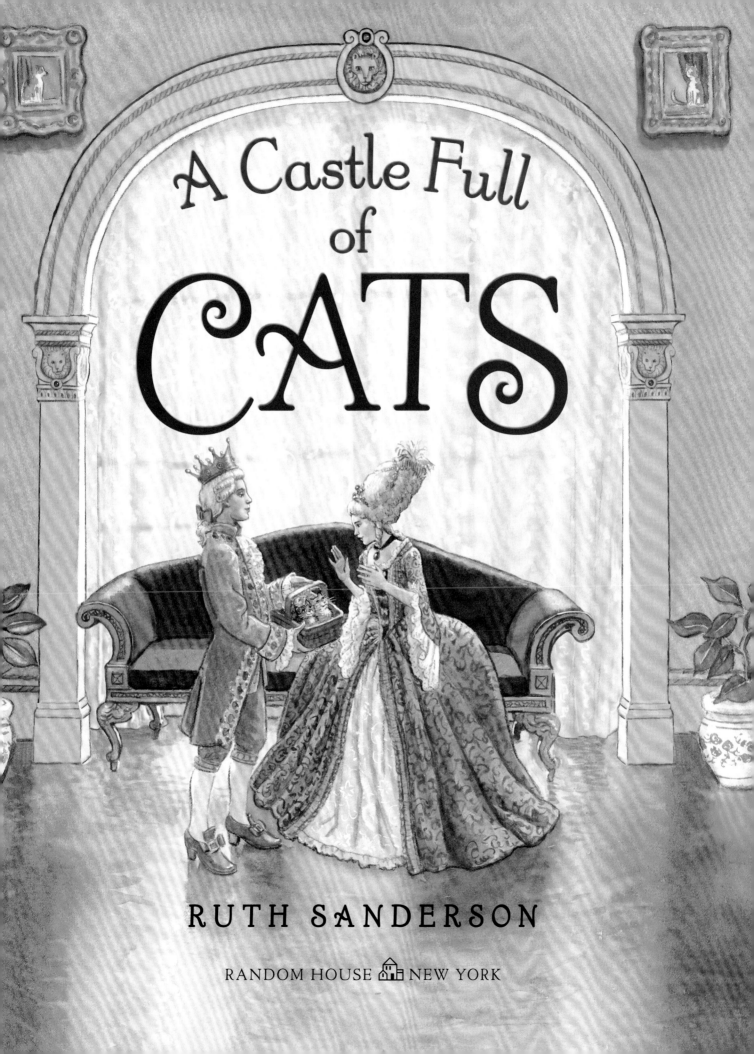

A Castle Full of CATS

RUTH SANDERSON

RANDOM HOUSE 🏠 NEW YORK

Library of Congress Cataloging-in-Publication Data
Sanderson, Ruth.
A castle full of cats / by Ruth Sanderson. — First edition.
pages cm.
Summary: The queen is devoted to her cats and they know they are loved,
but when they try to win the king's affection, they drive him right out of the castle—at least for a while.
ISBN 978-0-449-81307-2 (trade) — ISBN 978-0-375-97154-9 (lib. bdg.) — ISBN 978-0-375-98143-2 (ebook)
[1. Stories in rhyme. 2. Cats—Fiction. 3. Kings, queens, rulers, etc.—Fiction.] I. Title.

PZ8.3.S2243Cas 2015 [E]—dc23 2014012522

MANUFACTURED IN CHINA

10 9 8 7 6 5 4 3 2 1

First Edition

In memory of our beloved cats,
Sasha and Duke, who started it all

and thanks to everyone
who supplied me with photos to inspire
a castle full of cat characters

Once there was a queen
who kept a castle full of cats.

She loved the pretty ones and the plain ones,
the sweet ones and the brats.

The cats were spoiled and pampered—
they were the queen's delight.

They dined on fish for breakfast, lunch,
and dinner every night.

The cats had *her* affection—
they knew this to be true,

but now they had to find a way
to win the king's love, too.

They tried their best to please him
in oh-so-clever ways,

and left him charming little gifts
to brighten up his days.

They raced him down the hallway,
they scampered down the stairs,

and beat him to the parlor
to warm his favorite chairs.

The king loved art and music,
so the cats each did their part,
composing lovely serenades

and making works of art.

They sorted through his papers
and studied every book,
determined he would love them,
no matter what it took.

In spite of all their efforts,
they weren't his choice of pet.

"They're only being cats, my dear—
no need to get upset."

But the king had lost his patience.
"That's it! I've had enough!"
He dropped his spoon.
He grabbed his cane.
He marched off in a huff!

The queen peered out the window.
Cats perched on every chair.
They watched and waited many hours,
and then . . .

the king was there!

Is this the end of all our games?

The end to all our fun?

Or could it be, quite possibly . . .

Yes! The games have just begun!

Oh, what a purr-fect present!

And finally they knew
there was no longer any doubt . . .

the king *did* love them, too!

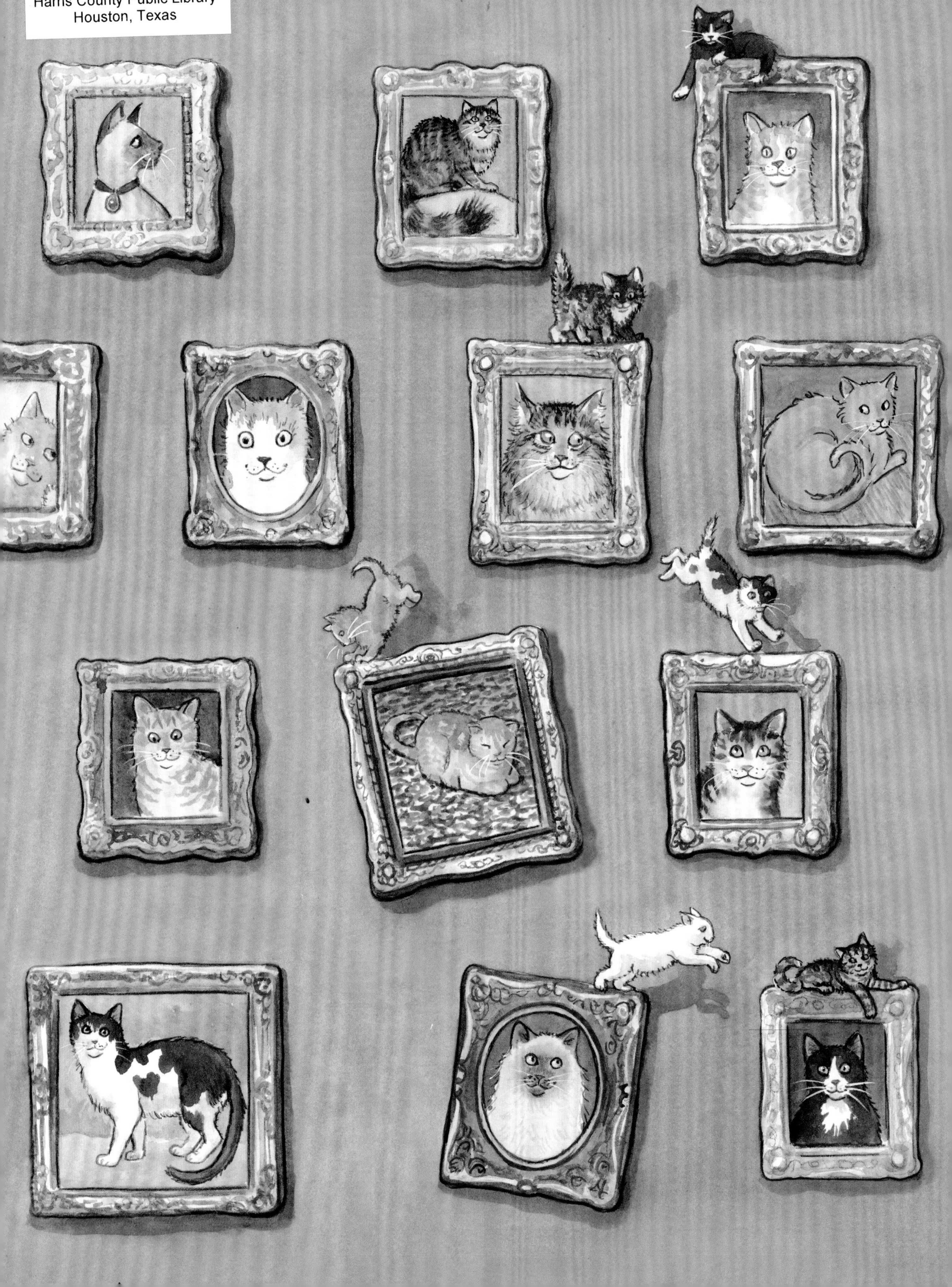